My 1st Classic Story

The Boy Who Cried Wolf

A retelling of Aesop's Fable
by Eric Blair

illustrated by Dianne Silverman

PICTURE WINDOW BOOKS
a capstone imprint

My First Classic Story is published by Picture Window Books
A Capstone Imprint
151 Good Counsel Drive, P.O. Box 669
Mankato, Minnesota 56002
www.capstonepub.com

Library of Congress Cataloging-in-Publication Data
Blair, Eric.
The boy who cried wolf: a retelling of Aesop's fable / retold by Eric Blair;
illustrated by Dianne Silverman.
p. cm. — (My first classic story)
Summary: A retelling of the fable in which a young boy's false cries for help
cause him problems when he is really in need of assistance.
ISBN 978-1-4048-6507-5 (library binding)
ISBN 978-1-4048-7364-3 (paperback)
[1. Fables. 2. Folklore.] I. Silverman, Dianne, ill. II. Aesop. III. Title. IV. Series.
PZ8.2.B595Bo 2011
398.2—dc22
[E]   2010050971

Art Director: Kay Fraser
Graphic Designer: Emily Harris
Production Specialist: Michelle Biedscheid

Printed in the United States of America in Stevens Point, Wisconsin.
092011   006366R

What Is a Fable?

A fable is a story that teaches a lesson. In some fables, animals may talk and act the way people do. A Greek slave named Aesop created some of the world's favorite fables. Aesop's fables have been enjoyed for more than 2,000 years.

Once upon a time, there was a young
shepherd boy.

Every morning, the boy led his father's sheep to an open field. There, the sheep grazed on grass.

The boy stayed in the lonely field with the sheep all day.

One day, the boy was bored. He decided to play a joke on the villagers.

He ran to the village and cried, "Wolf! Help! There is a wolf attacking my sheep!"

The villagers were kind. They left their work and came running to chase the wolf away.

But it was a trick.

Each time, the villagers came running. Each
time, there was no wolf.

One day, wolves really did attack the boy's sheep.

The boy was scared. He ran to the village and screamed, "Help! Wolves are attacking my sheep!"

But no one listened to the boy. No one came to help.

The villagers did not trust the boy, and the wolves ate his sheep.

Because the boy had lied so many times, nobody believed him, even when he was telling the truth.

23

The End